U.S. HOLIDAYS

Celebrate Presidents' Day

By Yvonne Pearson

PEBBLE
a capstone imprint

First Facts are published by Capstone Press,
1710 Roe Crest Drive, North Mankato, Minnesota 56003
www.mycapstone.com

Library of Congress Cataloging-in-Publication Data
Library of Congress Cataloging-in-Publication data is available on the Library of Congress website.
978-1-9771-0271-3 (library binding)
978-1-9771-0532-5 (paperback)
978-1-9771-0285-0 (eBook PDF)

Editorial Credits
Mandy Robbins, editor; Cynthia Della-Rovere, designer; Pam Mitsakos, media researcher; Tori Abraham, production specialist

Photo Credits
Alamy: Arina Habich, Cover (bottom), Ivy Close Images, 10-11; Getty Images: Bettmann 16-17; North Wind Picture Archives: 9; Shutterstock: Bokeh Blur Background, Design Element, David S Mohn, Cover (top), Duda Vasilii, Design Element, Everett Historical, 3 (bottom left), 6-7, 14-15, Masaki Norton, 12-13, Monkey Business Images, 20-21, Natalia Pushchina, 4-5, sharpner, 1 (bottom); The Image Works: Michael Geissinger, 18-19

Printed and bound in the United States of America.
PA49

Table of Contents

Celebrating Our Leaders

On Presidents' Day, Americans honor their presidents. Presidents have led the United States in good times. They have also guided the country through wars and disasters.

Presidents' Day also reminds people of their country. It gives everyone a chance to celebrate the United States of America.

The President of the United States lives in the White House.

How Presidents' Day Began

Presidents' Day began as a celebration of our first president, George Washington. He is the most famous leader in United States history. He led the military and the U.S. Colonies to win the ***Revolutionary War*** (1775-1783).

Fact George Washington is often called the father of our country.

revolution—an attempt to overthrow a government and replace it with a new system

Washington and his troops spent the winter of 1777–1778 in Valley Forge.

The Colonies won independence from Great Britain in 1783. But their new government was weak. State ***representatives*** created a stronger one. It called for a president. In 1789, Americans ***elected*** Washington.

After Washington died in 1799, people honored him on his birthday, February 22. It became a holiday.

representative—someone who is chosen to act or speak for others

elect—to choose someone as a leader by voting

Fact After the Revolutionary War, some Americans wanted Washington to be king. But he did not want that power. Washington went home to be a farmer.

Washington took the oath to become president in New York City in 1789.

In 1971 Congress changed Washington's birthday celebration to the third Monday of February. Lawmakers wanted to give ***federal*** workers a three-day weekend. Some Americans didn't like this. They wanted the holiday to stay on Washington's real birthday.

The Cherry Tree Story

In 1806 writer Mason Locke Weems told a story about Washington. He wanted to show that Washington was honest. The story says Washington chopped into his father's cherry tree when he was 6 years old. When his father asked him about it, he said, "I cannot tell a lie." But Weems made up the story. It's not really true.

Many artists have painted pictures that show the story of George Washington chopping his father's cherry tree.

federal—the central government of the United States

Honoring More Leaders

Many state leaders wanted to change George Washington's Birthday to Presidents' Day. Lawmakers in Washington's home state of Virginia disagreed. Today the holiday is known as Presidents' Day in many states. But its real name is still George Washington's Birthday.

From left to right, Mount Rushmore shows presidents George Washington, Thomas Jefferson, Theodore Roosevelt, and Abraham Lincoln.

Presidents' Day also honors President Abraham Lincoln. He led the country during the Civil War (1861-1865). Sadly, Lincoln was the first U.S. President to be killed in office.

Some states have a separate holiday for Lincoln's birthday. Others include it with George Washington's Birthday.

Fact Lincoln went to school for less than two years. He taught himself to be a lawyer.

President Lincoln visits his troops at City Point, Virginia, in 1865.

Today states celebrate the presidents in different ways. Alabama honors Washington and President Thomas Jefferson on Presidents' Day. Massachusetts has a separate day to honor presidents from New England. Indiana and Georgia celebrate Presidents' Day on December 24.

Daisy Gatson Bates

Arkansas celebrates two holidays on the third Monday in February. They are George Washington's Birthday and Daisy Gatson Bates Day. Bates was a ***civil rights*** leader from Arkansas. She played an important part in making sure kids of all races could go to school together.

Daisy Gatson Bates (right)

civil rights—the rights that all people have to freedom and equal treatment under the law

Many Ways to Celebrate

Americans hold big celebrations on Presidents' Day. The biggest parade is the George Washington Birthday Parade. It is held in Alexandria, Virginia. Around the country, people act out battle scenes or famous speeches from history. Washington's home, Mount Vernon, is free to visit on this day.

Fact Washington gave a Farewell Address when he stopped being president. A U.S. Senator reads it each year on George Washington's Birthday.

People dressed as Revolutionary War soldiers march in the George Washington Birthday Parade.

Students study the U.S. presidents at school. Some write letters to the president. Others pretend to run for president. These lessons help them understand what a president does.

Presidents' Day Sales

When Presidents' Day was moved to a Monday, it became a big day for shopping. In the 1970s, car dealers used the holiday as an opportunity to sell cars. Many other kinds of stores joined the holiday sales too. Today many Americans save money shopping during Presidents' Day sales.

The dog ran away
pro-noun
noun
Unit Family
Hundreds
Tens
100.0

Glossary

civil rights (SI-vil RYTS)—the rights that all people have to freedom and equal treatment under the law

elect (i-LEKT)—to choose someone as a leader by voting

federal (FED-ur-uhl)—the central government of the United States

representative (rep-ri-ZEN-tuh-tiv)—someone who is chosen to act or speak for others

revolution (rev-uh-LOO-shun)—an attempt to overthrow a government and replace it with a new system

Read More

Koestler-Grack, Rachel A. *Presidents' Day.* Celebrating Holidays. Minneapolis: Bellwether Media, Inc., 2018.

Meltzer, Brad. *I Am George Washington.* Ordinary People Change the World. New York: Dial Books for Young Readers, 2016.

Singer, Allison. *What Is the President's Job?* DK Readers. New York: DK Publishing, 2017.

Internet Sites

Use FactHound to find Internet sites related to this book.

Visit www.facthound.com

Just type in 9781977102713 and go.

Critical Thinking Questions

1. Why is George Washington called the father of our country?
2. Name two important things you learned about Abraham Lincoln.
3. Why was the celebration of George Washington's Birthday changed to the first Monday in February? Do you think it was a good idea?

Index